The Noise Lullaby

JACQUELINE K. OGBURN ☾ **JOHN SANDFORD**

LOTHROP, LEE & SHEPARD BOOKS   NEW YORK

To Ben, with love

J.K.O.

For Robin Johnson

J.S.

The illustrator wishes to thank Lane Ann Bayless, Roisin Moran, Eleanor Sandford, and Engine Block John Hayes for their gracious help in the preparation of this book.

Text copyright © 1995 by Jacqueline K. Ogburn
Illustrations copyright © 1995 by John Sandford
Inquiries should be addressed to Lothrop, Lee & Shepard Books,
a division of William Morrow & Company, Inc., 1350 Avenue of the Americas,
New York, New York 10019.
Printed in the United States of America.
First Edition   1 2 3 4 5 6 7 8 9 10
Library of Congress Cataloging in Publication Data
Ogburn, Jacqueline K. the noise lullaby / by Jacqueline K. Ogburn ; illustrated by John Sandford.
p.   cm.   Summary: Describes the noises a child hears at night before falling asleep.
ISBN 0-688-10452-5. — ISBN 0-688-10453-3 (lib.bdg.)
[1. Bedtime—Fiction. 2. Sound—Fiction.] I. Sandford, John.
1953- ill. II. Title. PZ7.03317No 1994 [E]—dc20
93-37417   CIP AC

*E*very night when I am in bed,
the world sings me a noise lullaby.

Some of the noises are outside noises.

Brumm, bruummm—*brruummmm.*
Bee-beep. EERRRROOOOMMM. Bee-*beeeep!*

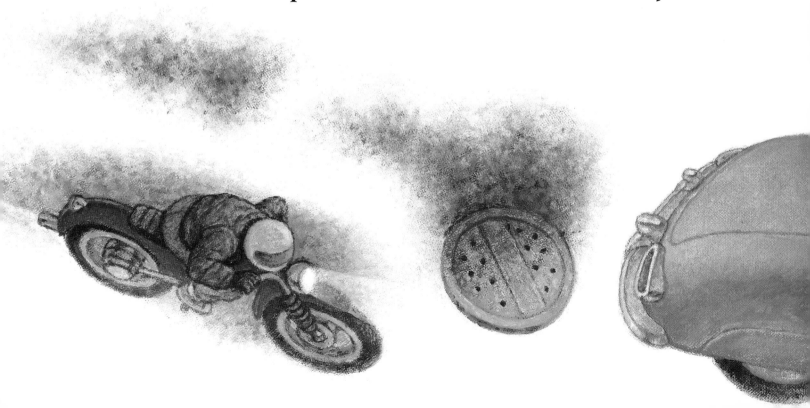

Crick-et, crick-et.

Katy-did, Katy-did, Katy-did-did-*did*.

Boom, chik-chik, a**BOOM**, chik-chik, a**BOOM**.

Wapa-wapa-wapa-wapa-**BOOM!**

Whoosh,

CRINKLE,

THUD, THUD,

Fooom - pa.

Some of the noises are inside noises.

thump . . .

blump,

thump,

blump,

Thump,

Ka-thunk, ra-rattle. Snik.

Erk-*eek*, erk-*eek*, erk-*eek*, erk-*eek*, erk-*eek*.
Rustle, rustle, russsss.

Klink, klink, **plonk.**
SSSSsssshhh. Bloop. *Swish, ssshhh.*

Klink!

Click.

UUuuuummmmmmmmm.

Tick, tick, tick, tick, tick, tick.

$\mathcal{S}$oon I will sing my own part in the noise lullaby.